First American edition published in 2001 by Carolrhoda Books, Inc.

Copyright © 2000 by Mark Birchall

Originally published in 2000 by Andersen Press Ltd., London, England,
under the title Rabbit's Woolly Jumper.

Carolrhoda Books, Inc.
A division of Lerner Publishing Group
241 First Avenue North, Minneapolis, MN 55401 U.S.A.

website address: www.lernerbooks.com

For Pip

Library of Congress Cataloging-in-Publication Data

Birchall, Mark, 1955–
Rabbit's wooly sweater / Mark Birchall. — 1st American ed.
p. cm.
Summary: Because she and her toy rabbit Mr. Cuddles always do
everything together, Rabbit does not want to wear her new sweater unless he has one as well.
ISBN 1–57505–465–5 (lib. bdg.)
[1. Sweaters – Fiction. 2. Rabbits – Fiction. 3. Toys – Fiction. 4. Behavior – Fiction.] Title.
PZ7.B51187Rab 2001 [E] – dc21 00 – 009035

Printed and bound in Italy
1 2 3 4 5 6 - OS - 05 04 03 02 01 00

Rabbit's Wooly Sweater

Mark Birchall

CAROLRHODA BOOKS, INC.
MINNEAPOLIS

Rabbit and Mr. Cuddles were best friends.
When Rabbit played on the swings, Mr. Cuddles
always went with her.

When Rabbit ate her dinner, Mr. Cuddles
always shared a bite.

And when Rabbit took a bath, Mr. Cuddles
always took one too.

Aunty Ethel came to visit.
"I knit you a present," she told Rabbit.
"Where's Mr. Cuddles's present?"
Rabbit asked. "He wants one just like mine."

"Mr. Cuddles doesn't need a wooly sweater,"
Mom said. "He has you to keep him warm."

Rabbit tried on the wooly sweater.

"It's too big," she grumbled. "Much too big."

"It's lovely," said Mom. "You can wear it to the park."

But Rabbit didn't want to wear it to the park.
If Mr. Cuddles didn't wear one, she didn't want to
wear one either, no matter how cold it was.

At the park, Rabbit pulled
off the wooly sweater.
When she took Mr. Cuddles to
play on the slide, she left the
wooly sweater on the ground.

When Rabbit played soccer, she used the wooly sweater as one of the goals.

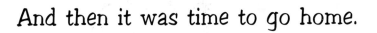

And then it was time to go home.

"What have you been doing with this?" Mom asked. "It's filthy. Put it in the washing machine."

The wooly sweater went around

and around

and around.

And as it went around, it shrank smaller

and smaller

and smaller.